FABIO
— THE WORLD'S GREATEST —
FLAMINGO DETECTIVE

PERIL AT LIZARD LAKE

LAURA JAMES

Illustrated by EMILY FOX

BLOOMSBURY
CHILDREN'S BOOKS
LONDON OXFORD NEW YORK NEW DELHI SYDNEY

BLOOMSBURY CHILDREN'S BOOKS
Bloomsbury Publishing Plc
50 Bedford Square, London WC1B 3DP, UK

BLOOMSBURY, BLOOMSBURY CHILDREN'S BOOKS and the Diana logo
are trademarks of Bloomsbury Publishing Plc

First published in Great Britain in 2020 by Bloomsbury Publishing Plc

A catalogue record for this book is available from the British Library

ISBN: PB: 978-1-4088-8937-4; eBook: 978-1-4088-8936-7

2 4 6 8 10 9 7 5 3 1

Typeset by Sue Mason

Printed in China by Leo Paper Products, Heshan, Guangdong

To find out more about our authors and books visit www.bloomsbury.com
and sign up for our newsletters

For Elena and Hannah – L.J.

For my studio buddies at Dove Street – E.F.

In a small town on the banks of Lake Laloozee lives the world's greatest flamingo detective. His name is **Fabio**. He's not tall or strong, but slight and pink. And he's very, very clever.

At his side for every case is his friend and associate, **Gilbert**, a giraffe terrible at the art of disguise but good at asking questions – sometimes even the right ones.

Chapter 1

Fabio walked wearily down Plume Street towards his office. The delights of his neighbourhood did not interest him that day.

He trudged up the stairs of his detective agency headquarters and entered to find Gilbert with his feet on the desk, reading the paper. Gilbert quickly put his feet back down on the floor.

LALOOZEE SWIMMING POOL
CLOSES
UNTIL FURTHER NOTICE

'Please tell me there's something interesting in that pile,' said Fabio, gesturing to the untidy stack of papers on Gilbert's desk.

'Slim pickings, I'm afraid,' replied Gilbert. 'There's a case of a missing umbrella.' Gilbert handed over the letter doubtfully. Fabio skim-read it and sighed.

'Reply to Mr Wild suggesting that, as he thinks he lost his umbrella on the bus, he might like to return to the depot and ask if it has been handed in to the lost and found.'

'Righto,' said Gilbert, making a note.

'What about that one?' asked Fabio, glancing over at a scrap of paper.

'That was a telephone message,' said Gilbert. 'I think we must be listed incorrectly in the directory because everyone who's rung up seems to need a plumber, not a detective.'

Brrrrring brrrrring.

'That'll be another one!' said Gilbert, rolling his eyes. Then in his best telephone voice, 'Office of the world's greatest flamingo detective, Gilbert speaking, how may I help you?'

Fabio took a stack of letters through to his office while Gilbert dealt with the enquiry. From the outer office he could hear Gilbert on the phone. His conversation sounded promising.

'... excellent! I'll head straight over. Thank you. Goodbye.'

Gilbert bounded into Fabio's office with a broad grin on his face.

Fabio stood up eagerly. 'A new case? Fit for the world's greatest flamingo detective?'

'Well, no, not exactly,' said Gilbert, a

little crestfallen. 'But I think you're going to like it. Something very exciting has just arrived. How would you like a day out of the office?'

'That sounds like a splendid idea,' replied Fabio, reaching for his hat. 'Lead the way, my friend.'

It wasn't long before they were racing through the streets of Laloozee in Gilbert's sports car. Gilbert was bursting to tell Fabio the surprise.

He wasn't very good at keeping secrets, so it was taking quite a lot of effort not to give the game away.

They took the road out of town for about a mile and then swung left on to a dirt track. Fabio shut his eyes and held on to his hat until the car came to a stop.

'I bet you can't guess where we are!' said Gilbert, barely containing his excitement.

Fabio opened his eyes. 'An airfield,' he said decisively.

'How on earth did you guess that?' asked Gilbert, forgetting that Fabio

was something of an expert at making educated guesses.

'It was easy,' replied Fabio. 'Flat land, a big shed that could easily be an aircraft hangar and finally –' Fabio pointed – 'a windsock.'

'Oh,' sighed Gilbert. 'Nothing gets

past you. Well, you'll never guess what I've bought!'

'A submarine?' asked Fabio, with a twinkle in his eye.

'No! That would be … oh, ha ha, very funny,' replied Gilbert, realising he was being teased.

'Is it a plane, my friend?'

'Well, as a matter of fact, it is,' said Gilbert. 'Do you want to come and see it?'

Gilbert proudly led Fabio to the hangar and pulled back the doors to reveal a small silver biplane.

'Isn't she a beauty?' he said, grinning. 'I'm calling her Angel. Here, grab some goggles and hop in.'

With Gilbert's help, Fabio climbed on to the wing and then into the front seat of the plane. Once he was safely strapped in, Gilbert took his place in the pilot's seat.

'I didn't know you'd flown in one of these before,' said Fabio.

'Well, I haven't exactly,' confessed Gilbert. 'But the stork who sold it to me taught me the basics – forward, up, down, that sort of thing. He flew her in from the Coral Coast this morning. That was him calling the office. He said it's all very simple really. Logical, even. You'll like it, Fabio, I promise.'

Gilbert started the engines. 'Ready?'

'What, you mean … ?' But Fabio's voice was drowned out by the sound of the propellers starting and before he knew what was happening they were taxiing out of the hangar. At the top of the runway Gilbert tapped Fabio on the shoulder and gave him the thumbs up. Despite himself, Fabio did the same. But as Gilbert increased the throttle

and they prepared for take-off, Fabio suddenly yearned for that quiet day in the office.

Their plane bumped off the ground once, and then again. The end of the runway and some very tall trees were rapidly getting closer.

'Up she goes!' cheered Gilbert, oblivious of any danger, and their little plane took to the air.

'Well, that wasn't too difficult,' he commented as Fabio noticed the wheels clipping branches below them.

'I won't try anything fancy like a loop the loop on our first trip out,' shouted Gilbert over the noise of the engine, as he levelled the plane.

'That's very good of you, Gilbert,' Fabio called back, but to his surprise he was enjoying himself.

The savannah stretched out below them. It was mostly lush grassland with the occasional settlement. The reflection of the morning sun twinkled on a tiny river as it meandered towards Laloozee.

Fabio hadn't realised that flying

would suit him so well. He was about to tell Gilbert how much fun he was having when the engine spluttered. 'What was that?' he asked.

'Um, nothing,' called Gilbert, frantically looking at the instruments in front of him for clues.

The engine spluttered again.

'Gilbert? Did the stork who sold you

the plane refuel after flying all the way from the Coral Coast?' Fabio yelled back.

Gilbert's eyes finally found the fuel gauge just as the engine stopped completely. 'It appears we have run out of fuel,' Gilbert shouted. But he had no need to, as they were suddenly flying in eerie silence. 'Well, at least we can hear each other properly,' he joked, trying to stay positive.

'Didn't you check the fuel gauge before we took off?' asked Fabio.

'I didn't know I was supposed to,' replied Gilbert weakly.

'How did you think it stayed up in the air?'

As if on cue, the nose of the plane started to dive.

'Pull up!' shouted Fabio, as panic began to set in.

Gilbert wrestled the plane into a glide, but they were rapidly losing altitude.

Fabio scanned the ground below, looking for a safe place to land.

'There!' he said, pointing to a clearing.

'I see it!' shouted Gilbert, as the ground got closer and closer.

Gilbert tried his best to follow Fabio's instructions and guide the small plane towards his suggested landing site. It wasn't easy.

'Hold tight!' he called out as they

connected with the ground. They bounced on touchdown before hitting the earth a second time, wing first. As it scraped along the ground, sparks flying, the wing acted as a brake and finally they stopped.

'Thank goodness this clearing was here!' said Gilbert cheerfully.

Eventually the dust settled and Fabio opened his eyes. He removed his goggles and looked around, a chill running down his spine. They were being watched.

Chapter 2

A lioness in oil-stained overalls stepped out of the undergrowth. 'Did you intend to do that?' she asked, cool as you like.

'Well, not exactly,' confessed Gilbert. 'Bit of trouble with the fuel.'

'Are you a mechanic, by any chance?' asked Fabio.

'I am, as it happens,' replied the lioness with a proud smile. 'The only one for miles around. This must be your lucky day.

My name's Molly,' she added.

'Fabio, at your service, madam,' Fabio introduced himself. 'And this is my good friend Gilbert.'

'Pleased to meet you,' said Gilbert.

'I can take a look at your plane if you like,' replied Molly. 'And you can freshen up in the village.'

Gilbert climbed out of the mangled fuselage and helped Fabio down. 'Do you really think you can fix the plane for us?' asked Gilbert, scratching his head doubtfully.

'I've seen worse,' she said. 'Follow me, I'll take you into the village.'

Soon they came to the main street. The whole place was decorated with streamers and bunting.

'Is there a festival going on?' asked Fabio.

'Yes, in two days' time we're celebrating Sun Day,' replied Molly.

'I thought it was Friday in two days' time,' whispered Gilbert.

'It's actually Saturday,' Fabio corrected him. 'But I'd say, looking at those yellow and orange discs, that the festival is celebrating the sun.'

'Like the one in the sky?' asked Gilbert.

'The very same,' smiled Fabio.

Molly directed them to a garage next to a cafe.

'Is this your garage?' asked Gilbert.

'Looks like it,' she laughed,

pointing to the sign above the door.

Because the remote village wasn't used to visitors, Fabio and Gilbert had already drawn a small crowd. Gilbert entertained the kids with a game of hide-and-seek while Molly showed Fabio to her office to discuss the plane.

'There's a customer at pump four, Arthur,' she said as she strode in. A hunched armadillo hastily covered up something on his desk and scurried out to the forecourt.

'He's very shy,' said Molly, chuckling. 'It's always the quiet ones you have to look out for.'

Fabio took in his surroundings and Molly followed his gaze. 'That was the first car I ever worked on,' she said, pointing to a picture on the wall. It was a photograph of a rally car, mid-race.

'My dad told me it was only good for scrap, that car,' Molly told him, 'but said I could have it if I really wanted it. She ran like a dream in the end. Helped me to become a champion rally driver by the time I was fourteen.' Molly showed Fabio

her impressive trophy cabinet.

'You must have been very dedicated,' remarked Fabio.

'I was,' Molly agreed, clearing her desk of a set of drawings.

'Are they designs for another car?' he asked.

'Oh, no,' said Molly. 'This is another project.'

'Do you still race?' asked Fabio.

'Not since the accident,' replied Molly. 'The car was a write-off and my co-driver moved on.'

'I see,' said Fabio. 'I'm sorry to hear that.'

'You ask a lot of questions,' observed Molly. 'Are you a tax inspector?'

'I'm sorry,' replied Fabio with a laugh. 'I'm a detective. I want to know the answer to everything. Usually it's Gilbert who asks a lot of questions.'

Molly seemed keen to change the subject. 'Now, what about that plane of his …'

Once the finer points of the repairs were agreed, Fabio went in search of Gilbert.

It didn't take him long to locate his friend. Just by a petrol pump a long giraffe-shaped shadow fell at his feet. Fabio smiled and beckoned over a young mongoose, whose turn it was to 'seek'.

'I think I may have found what you've been looking for,' he said, pointing to the ground.

The mongoose squealed in delight and his friends came running.

'We can see you, Gilbert!' they laughed.

'What? No!' said Gilbert from his hiding place. 'How did you know I was here?'

'Because they're very, very clever!' replied Fabio.

Gilbert came out from his hiding place, arms raised in mock surrender. 'You got me!' he said.

As the kids ran off to play another game, Gilbert turned to Fabio. 'I say, all this hide-and-seek makes one rather thirsty.'

Fabio could see it was time for a drink. 'I wonder whether we might find ourselves a cool glass of pink lemonade in the cafe next door.'

The cafe was called Mungo's. There they were greeted by a friendly scorpion by the name of Gertie. She showed them to a table on the terrace and took their order.

When their drinks arrived, Fabio raised his glass. 'To safe landings, my friend!'

'I'll drink to that,' replied Gilbert, taking a gulp.

'We'll all be drinking pink lemonade soon,' said a gazelle sitting at a nearby table.

'Well, it is delicious,' said Gilbert.

'Not for that reason,' replied the

gazelle. 'The water here seems to be running out.'

'Running out?' asked Fabio.

'Yes,' said the gazelle. 'The trouble began just this week, but now we turn the taps on and get only a trickle.'

Fabio narrowed his eyes the way he did when he knew something out of the ordinary was happening, and his mind went back to all the plumbing enquiries they'd received that morning. Perhaps there hadn't been a mistake in the directory after all.

'I'm worried for my patients,' the

gazelle informed them.

'Are you a doctor?' asked Gilbert.

'Yes, Ginger's my name. I've been the local doctor here for twenty years. I've never seen anything like this water shortage.'

'Luckily for you, Ginger,' said Gilbert, 'Fabio here is the world's greatest flamingo detective. I'm sure he can solve the problem.'

'A real detective?' asked Ginger just as Mungo, the proprietor of the cafe, came to clear the empty glasses.

'Don't you go worrying our guests,

Ginger,' said the scorpion, wiping the table. 'We've got that wonderful new bottled water, "Mm", now. I've been selling lots of it this week.' Mungo showed them a bottle which had been left on another table.

Fabio felt sure he'd seen the logo before.

'This is wrong!' exclaimed Ginger. 'We need water from our taps. We shouldn't have to buy it in bottles. You'll look into it, won't you, Fabio? We simply can't let this happen.'

'I'd be delighted to solve this mystery

for you,' replied Fabio with a smile. Finally the world's greatest flamingo detective was back on the case.

'Seems like everyone thinks you're a plumber now,' noted Gilbert.

Chapter 3

Fabio and Gilbert started their investigations by going door to door, asking questions. It soon became clear that everyone in the village was affected by the lack of water. After a conversation with an elephant who was afraid his window-cleaning business would fail if the water didn't come back, Fabio made a decision.

'We need to go to the source,' he said, looking into the distance.

'Gilbert, we're going to the Black Mountains.'

At Molly's garage, Fabio and Gilbert found Arthur working under the bonnet of a truck. 'Hello, Arthur. We need to borrow one of your trucks, to go up into the mountains,' said Fabio.

Arthur scrambled out from beneath the vehicle. 'You can take this one if you like,' he said. 'I've just fixed her.'

'What are you doing?' asked an angry voice.

It was Molly on her way back from Mungo's cafe.

'They want to borrow a truck,' replied Arthur nervously. 'I thought this one would be best.'

'That old thing? You must be mad!'

Arthur shut the door of the truck with a little more force than was necessary.

Molly ignored him. 'What do you want

it for?' she asked Fabio.

'We're going to work out why there's no water in the village,' he replied. 'We need to head up into the Black Mountains to find the source.'

'It's very dangerous on the mountain road,' Molly warned them.

Gilbert explained that he was a very good driver.

'All right then, you can take my truck,' said Molly, even though she didn't seem convinced.

'But –'

'Oh, do be quiet, Arthur,' said Molly,

interrupting him. 'Go and bring my truck round.'

Arthur sulkily did as he was told, and when he'd brought it round, Molly had a quick look under the bonnet.

'It's very dangerous on that road,' she said, handing Gilbert the keys.

'So you mentioned,' replied Gilbert, taking the keys and climbing into the cabin. He felt sure he was up to the job.

'She's got a full tank,' Molly informed him.

Gilbert sighed. No one was going to let him forget running out of fuel.

They waved as they drove off. Fabio frowned. He had a strong feeling that Molly had tried to put them off going.

'Shall we listen to the radio?' asked Gilbert, tuning in to the local station, The Zee. It was coming to the end of the news bulletin.

'Just to repeat our warnings, the water has now run out in the whole of the Laloozee area. Local officials are recommending that people use Lake Laloozee for washing and buy bottled water for drinking. We'll have an update for you in half an hour on this breaking story. Now for the latest record by Julia the jazz-singing hippo and her band …'

'Oh, I like this one,' said Gilbert, starting to jig in his seat.

But Fabio couldn't concentrate on the beautiful music. As they headed out of the village, he felt sure this was no simple drought, but something far more sinister.

Chapter 4

The road up to the Black Mountains was more like a track, and it clung precariously to the mountainside. There was only enough room for one vehicle. On Fabio's side the truck skimmed the rock face. On Gilbert's side there was a sheer drop into a ravine.

Gilbert was getting neck ache. He missed his sports car with its open roof.

Up ahead the road opened out and the land plateaued. Ahead of them was

Lizard Lake, the source of water for the whole Laloozee area.

'It's funny to see a lake all the way up here,' commented Gilbert.

'Don't you remember your geography?' asked Fabio. 'This is a glacial lake, formed many thousands of years ago.'

'Is it?' asked Gilbert. 'I didn't take geography at school. A girl in the class used to bully me, so I took needlework instead. She was a mean little –'

'The lake looks healthy enough to me,' Fabio interrupted him, keen as he was to focus on the job at hand. 'But we'll take a walk along the shoreline anyway. We might find some clues.'

Fabio's plans were frustrated by the rocky ground. 'It's a shame we can't walk further,' he sighed, dabbing his forehead with his handkerchief.

Gilbert sat on a rock by the water's edge and started doing exercises to stretch out his neck.

At that moment something shiny caught Fabio's eye. He moved closer to take a look. Dusting off some earth, he was surprised to see an empty glass bottle. On it was the same heart-shaped logo he'd seen at Mungo's cafe. 'This is Mm water,' said Fabio. 'What is it doing here?'

'Perhaps someone wanted a drink?' asked Gilbert.

'Gilbert, there's a whole lake full of water here. I'm beginning to think the village is suffering from no natural drought. I believe someone is stealing the water from this lake and selling it back to the villagers, the very people the water shortage is leaving thirsty! What we need to do is find out how … and who.'

He examined the bottle thoughtfully.

'You know, Gilbert, I'm sure I've seen this logo somewhere before Mungo's cafe.'

'He did say they sold it at Molly's garage – perhaps you saw it there,' replied Gilbert.

'At Molly's garage ...' mused Fabio, retracing the first time he went there in his mind. Suddenly his eyes widened in realisation. 'When I walked into Molly's office, Arthur quickly covered up something on his desk. I glimpsed what he was drawing, Gilbert. It was a heart.'

'You don't think Arthur is behind all this, do you?' asked Gilbert. 'Quiet Arthur?'

'I don't know,' replied Fabio. 'But I'm sure he knows more than he's letting on. Come on, we need to head back to the garage. We've got questions to ask.'

'Now, I want you to drive slowly,' said Fabio as they climbed back into the truck.

'I'm a very good driver!' moaned Gilbert. 'Why won't anyone believe me?'

'It's not that, my friend,' replied Fabio. 'If my thoughts are on the right lines, the ravine will be practically empty. I need to check.'

Gilbert carefully drove them down the mountain road while Fabio leaned out of his window to look into the ravine.

'What can you see?' asked Gilbert.

'It's difficult to see anything,' replied Fabio. 'There are too many rocks and trees in the way. Further ahead should be better.'

Gilbert drove on and suddenly it became clear to Fabio that the ravine was empty.

'The water's gone, Gilbert. Stop here, so I can take a better look,' he ordered.

But instead of stopping, the truck was picking up speed as the slope got steeper.

'Stop, Gilbert! We need to find out where the water is going.'

'Um, Fabio?' Gilbert said, frantically pressing the brake pedal. The truck was rolling faster.

'Didn't you hear me, Gilbert? I said slow down!'

'I would if I could!' replied Gilbert. 'But the brakes have gone!'

They suddenly found themselves hurtling down the mountain. Ahead of them was a sharp bend, which they took at breakneck speed. Gilbert hauled on the steering wheel and just managed to stay on the road, but the force flung open Fabio's door, leaving Fabio clinging to it by his wing tips and dangling over the ravine.

'Hang on!' shouted Gilbert, trying to reach out to his friend as he steered one-handed around another hairpin bend.

Ahead of them was a tunnel.

'Fabio!' cried Gilbert, and with one

enormous lunge he managed to pull his friend back into the safety of the truck's cabin. A second later Fabio's door struck the rocks at the entrance to the tunnel and crashed down into the ravine.

The impact slowed the truck down a little, and as the road levelled out Gilbert used the handbrake to bring them to a complete stop at the base of the mountain.

'You saved my life, my friend!' said Fabio, giving him a hug.

'I told you I was a good driver!' replied Gilbert.

'Even so,' said Fabio, his feathers a little ruffled, 'I suggest we walk back to the village. I won't take any more risks in that truck. I suspect those brakes did not sabotage themselves. And whose job was it to check those brakes, Gilbert?'

Gilbert gasped. 'Arthur!'

Chapter 5

Back at Molly's garage, Fabio and Gilbert found Arthur in the office.

'We've just had a close call up on that mountain, no thanks to you,' said Gilbert.

Arthur looked really alarmed. 'Why, what happened?'

'The brakes failed!' Gilbert's voice had gone a little squeaky.

'Let me handle this, Gilbert,' said Fabio, taking control of the situation.

'Show me what you were drawing when I first came into this office.'

'It was nothing,' replied Arthur, looking extremely guilty.

'Show me,' demanded Fabio.

Reluctantly, from under a pile of invoices and order forms for the garage, Arthur revealed his drawings. Fabio saw instantly that they were indeed pictures of hearts, but not designs for the bottled-water logo. They were designs for heart-shaped sunglasses.

'I'm hoping to become a designer,' Arthur explained. 'I'm planning on selling

these at the Sun Day festival. Please
don't tell Molly. She'll fire me if she finds
out I've been designing sunglasses on
company time.'

'I see,' said Fabio.

'I'm sorry about your journey up
into the mountains,' Arthur continued.

'Molly should have let you borrow the other truck. I'd just finished working on it. Molly insists on doing all the work on her own truck, so I'm surprised there was a problem with the brakes. She's an excellent mechanic.'

'I'm sorry for troubling you, Arthur,' said Fabio. 'We'll leave you to your work now. Your secret's safe with us.'

As they left the garage, Fabio caught Gilbert's arm. 'Gilbert,' he said. 'Our only lead has come to nothing and the villagers still need water. We'll head back to Lake Laloozee in your plane so that we can bring them back supplies.'

'Oh!' said Gilbert. 'Yes, I suppose we should do that. We don't seem to be getting anywhere with our investigations. Maybe this case is too difficult even for you to solve?'

Fabio didn't answer directly, he just patted his friend's shoulder. 'I shall go and supervise the final stage of the repairs,' he said. 'Meet me at the airfield in an hour.'

Gilbert lost three rounds of hide-and-seek with the village children before making his way to the runway. There he met Fabio, who was already donning flying goggles, and Molly, who was proudly leaning against his beautiful plane.

'Is my Angel better?' Gilbert asked, like a concerned father.

'She is,' said Molly with a smile, 'although you might notice some small changes. You can see,' she pointed out, 'that I've managed to straighten out the propeller and I've reshaped the metal panels on the wing and fuselage.'

Gilbert couldn't believe his eyes. 'Ah, my little Angel,' he exclaimed, hugging the plane. 'You're all better … and –' he looked down, baffled – 'you've got shoes on!'

'They're for landing on Lake Laloozee,' said Fabio. 'I asked Molly and Arthur to convert her into a seaplane. And Arthur has painted this angel on the side for good luck.'

'You're amazing!' said Gilbert. 'Thank you so much.'

'So you're going back to Laloozee, eh?' asked Molly. 'I'm sure this whole water problem will have sorted itself out soon enough.'

'Molly, you sound like you're pleased to see the back of us,' joked Gilbert.

'Not at all, not at all,' laughed Molly,

tapping the side of the plane with her paw. 'Don't worry,' she added. 'I filled up the fuel tank for you.'

Gilbert nodded his thanks.

When they were ready to leave, Arthur handed Gilbert a tin.

Gilbert had a quick peek inside. 'Sandwiches!' he said. 'That's very kind of you, Arthur.' He put the tin safely in the cockpit.

'We'll telephone you from Lake Laloozee,' said Fabio as he tipped his hat to Molly and Arthur and climbed in. 'And fly back with supplies as soon as possible.'

'I'm sure there'll be no need,' said Molly, waving them off.

They stood well back as Gilbert started the engine. 'Ready?' he asked.

Fabio nodded.

Gilbert manoeuvred the plane to the top of the makeshift runway. The ground was rocky and uneven. It wouldn't be an easy take-off for an experienced pilot, let alone one with less than a day's flying time.

'You can do this, Gilbert,' Fabio reassured his friend. 'Just make sure we leave the ground before we hit those rocks!'

'Good idea!' shouted Gilbert over the noise of the propeller.

The plane jostled over the uneven terrain. Fabio made some quick calculations in his head, distance divided by speed, and then crossed his feathers.

'You're going too far to the left, Gilbert,' Fabio shouted. 'Straighten her up!'

Gilbert muttered something about front-seat drivers but did as he was told, and amazingly they became airborne.

Gilbert dipped the wing of the plane in thanks to Molly and Arthur.

'Now, Naughty Elephants Squirt Water,' recited Gilbert, trying to work out the right direction for Laloozee.

'It's that way!' shouted Fabio, pointing ahead.

'No! Surely it's this way!' argued Gilbert over the noise of the propellers.

'You are right, my friend. Lake Laloozee is that way, but we're not heading there. We're heading for the Black Mountains,' replied Fabio.

'But I thought –'

'It was a trick, my friend,' said Fabio. 'I didn't want anyone from the village to know where we were really going.'

'You could have told me!' said Gilbert.

'Gilbert, you're terrible at keeping secrets!'

'Fair point.'

Once Gilbert had set their course for the Black Mountains, he offered Fabio one of Arthur's sandwiches.

As he handed one forward Fabio asked, 'Do you hear something?'

'I can't hear much over the sound of the engine,' replied Gilbert. 'Oh, look!' he added. 'How sweet – Arthur's written us a note.' Gilbert took the folded piece of paper from the tin, but it slipped from his grasp.

'I'm sure I hear something,' shouted Fabio, but Gilbert was distracted trying to catch the note. 'Gilbert, I'm afraid someone's noticed our change of course.'

But still Gilbert was not listening. Instead, triumphantly he shouted, 'Got it! It reads …'

'We're being followed.'

'No. It doesn't say that,' said Gilbert. 'It says …'

Chapter 6

Fabio looked behind them. Silhouetted against the clouds was another plane. It seemed to be following them.

'Who do you think it is?' asked Gilbert.

'Molly, of course,' said Fabio, seizing the controls and tilting them sharply back, making the plane climb almost vertically into the clouds.

'Whoa!' cried Gilbert. 'And you think I'm a crazy driver.'

'We're hiding,' said Fabio.

Molly's plane was now directly below them.

'Why is she following us?' asked Gilbert.

'She wanted to make sure we were heading back to town,' replied Fabio as he dramatically decreased their altitude until they were flying exactly above her.

Then he dipped the plane even lower.

Molly shook her paw at them but was forced to move down in order not to be hit.

'Any lower and she'll have to land,' shouted Gilbert.

'That's what I'm hoping,' Fabio shouted back.

The Black Mountains loomed ahead. Molly had to act. She bore left, narrowly avoiding the side of a mountain but causing her plane to stall. The plane spiralled into a nosedive.

Gilbert gulped but Molly ejected and released her parachute with just seconds to spare. Her plane ploughed into the mountainside and exploded on impact.

Fabio and Gilbert watched on as the lioness, still angrily lashing her tail, landed on the valley floor.

'She seemed so nice,' reflected Gilbert, peering down.

'Look, Gilbert, there's the ravine!' Fabio pointed to a change in the terrain below them. Ahead, the sunlight reflected on Lizard Lake. 'We need to be on the lookout for something out of the ordinary. There's some way they are stopping the water flowing into the ravine. Now we're in the air we should be able to see it.'

'Over there!' said Gilbert. 'What's that?'

Fabio took a look. Where a waterfall used to be, someone had built a dam.

It was time to land.

Gilbert took back the controls and circled Angel around the lake, to approach from the far side.

Fabio held his breath, unsure if the repaired plane would cope with the landing.

'Here goes!' shouted Gilbert as he prepared for landing.

The plane hit the water with a smack and there was a moment where Fabio feared they might flip over completely, but it was all right. They came to a stop in the centre of the lake.

'Now what?' asked Gilbert.

'Now we swim,' replied Fabio.

'But I don't like getting my ears wet,' replied Gilbert.

'You won't get your ears wet,' Fabio assured him.

Of course, things were much better for Fabio, who clung on to Gilbert's neck while he paddled to the dam.

It didn't take Gilbert long to realise he was in the shallows and could walk. Fabio refused to climb down until they were well and truly back on dry land.

When they reached the dam wall, Gilbert rested against it and wrung out the water in his cravat. Fabio turned and gazed out over the sheer drop into the dry ravine below. When he turned back, Gilbert was gone.

'Gilbert?'

Fabio looked at the spot where Gilbert had just been standing.

'Gilbert?' he asked again.

'There must be a trapdoor,' he reasoned. He started pushing against the stones.

Suddenly, he was gone too, as a stone gave way under his wing and he fell through the wall into darkness. He landed on Gilbert.

'There you are!' he said.

'And there you are!' came a voice.

Fabio and Gilbert peered into the gloom. A shadow on the wall revealed the unmistakeable silhouette of a scorpion.

It was Mungo.

Chapter 7

'There's no point my pretending to be nice now, I suppose,' said Mungo, who had lost his congenial cafe-owner's manner. 'Welcome to the manufacturing headquarters of Mm water,' he declared with a proud grin. 'We have control of the water supply for this whole region,' he smiled. 'Soon everyone from here to Laloozee will be begging us to sell them our bottled water.'

Giant Mm logos loomed over them.

It seemed so strange to Fabio that this heart shape was the symbol of such a heartless organisation.

Mungo herded Fabio and Gilbert into a tunnel which opened out into a large cavern. It was the nerve centre of the operation. The walls were covered with maps, showing the land all the way down to Lake Laloozee.

'Our water empire!' boasted Mungo.

'The water's not yours to take,' Fabio challenged him. 'You're a thief. You and Molly should be ashamed of …' He trailed off as he noticed Mungo's tail aligned perfectly with half of the heart-shaped logo on the wall.

'Molly?!' said a voice. 'You think that overgrown kitten could think up a scheme like this?'

The menacing figure of an even larger scorpion filled the exit to the cavern, and as she stood next to Mungo their tails formed the perfect heart shape.

Fabio could feel Gilbert start to shake next to him.

'The name's Margot, by the way,' said the second scorpion as a small drop of poison fell from the tip of her tail. 'Have you fellas got any last words?'

'You know I told you about the girl who bullied me in geography class ...' whispered Gilbert.

'Margot?' asked Fabio.

'Margot,' confirmed Gilbert.

To Gilbert's complete surprise, Fabio started congratulating them. 'What a genius scheme,' he said. 'I have to say, you had me fooled.'

'Not much of a detective, are you?' mocked Mungo.

'It was an ingenious plan!' Fabio continued. 'Do tell us how you came up with it,' he encouraged them. 'Was it your idea, Mungo?'

'It certainly was not!' Margot stepped in before Mungo had a chance to reply.

'It was!' protested Mungo. 'I am the brains behind this operation.'

'You are not! You barely have a brain. If it wasn't for me, you'd still be living with Mum and she'd be washing your socks.'

'Margot's his sister!' exclaimed Gilbert, putting two and two together. But the brother and sister were no longer paying attention to their captives. Fabio had cleverly managed to ignite a full-blown sibling argument.

'Right, that's it!' said Mungo, going for his sister, which was a mistake, as she was clearly much stronger than he was.

Margot reached for one of the Mm bottles and threw it at Mungo. It shattered on the cavern floor.

As the pair circled each other, Fabio looked at the system of levers and pulleys that controlled the dam's sluice gates.

'Why don't we just pull them all?' suggested Gilbert.

'We have to be careful not to flood the valley,' Fabio told him. Slowly, he pulled the three levers. 'That should be enough to restore the water supply.' They could both now hear the sound of rushing water as the sluice gates opened.

Meanwhile, Mungo and Margot's row
had escalated.

'You're always bossing me around!'
Mungo was saying.

'You're a little squirt,' replied Margot.

Mungo went to push Margot but slipped and lost his footing. As he did so, he grabbed hold of his sister to keep his balance. She was so surprised she too fell, taking them both down the sluice gate like a water slide.

Margot reached the end of the sluice and clung on, battling against the torrent of water, but Mungo couldn't stop. He barrelled into her and sent them both over the edge and into the ravine.

Chapter 8

Fabio and Gilbert carefully made their way back across the water to Gilbert's Angel.

'May I?' asked Fabio as he climbed in.

'Be my guest,' said Gilbert with a smile.

Fabio started the engine and proceeded to make an immaculate take-off. As they rose in the air Gilbert looked down.

'Oh look, it's Chief Inspector Duff!'

'So it is,' said Fabio. 'I called him from Molly's office and suggested he might be needed up here at Lizard Lake.'

Duff was driving carefully on the mountain road. In the back of his van was Molly, looking very angry.

As Fabio and Gilbert flew over the ravine, they could see Mungo and Margot bobbing along in the river. Gilbert waved at them.

'How does it feel to get one up on your school bully?' asked Fabio.

'Very good indeed!' replied Gilbert.

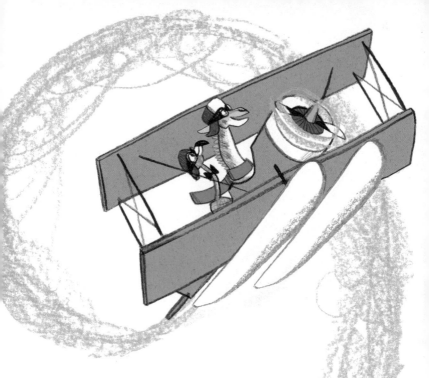

'Ready for a loop the loop?'
asked Fabio.

'Always!' cheered Gilbert.

'On behalf of the village,' began Ginger, 'I'd like us to raise our glasses to Fabio and Gilbert for successfully returning water to our taps!'

'To Fabio and Gilbert!' everyone cheered.

'I say,' said Gilbert. 'This is very good pink lemonade, Ginger.'

'Fabio gave me his old family recipe,' Ginger replied with a smile.

Fabio and Gilbert took a stroll through the village, admiring the effort everyone had put into the Sun Day celebrations.

At Arthur's stall Gilbert bought himself

a pair of heart-shaped sunglasses. They were proving to be very popular. He put them on. 'Can you still recognise me?' he asked Fabio.

'Of course, my friend,' replied Fabio. They were not a very good disguise.

Fabio stopped when they came to Molly's garage. 'There's just one thing I need to check,' he said.

Gilbert followed him into Molly's office and found him looking at a photograph on the wall.

'See this?' said Fabio. 'This was taken of Molly when she was a rally-car driver.'

Gilbert looked at the picture of the rally car mid-air, mid-race. 'Looks exciting!'

'It's partially in shadow, but can you see who her co-driver is?'

'It's Margot!' exclaimed Gilbert.

'Indeed it is,' said Fabio. 'They go back a long way, so when Margot needed someone clever enough to build a dam, she knew just who to turn to.'

'When did you suspect that Molly was involved?' he asked Fabio.

'Well, I was suspicious of her from the start,' said Fabio. 'But I had no evidence against her. All the evidence seemed to point to ...'

'Poor Arthur,' said Gilbert.

'Exactly,' said Fabio. 'Arthur became suspicious of her when she made sure we took her truck up to the mountains, knowing full well the brakes weren't good.'

'Thank goodness I'm such a good driver!' said Gilbert.

Fabio smiled at his friend. 'After that I decided it wasn't safe to let her know we were going back to Lizard Lake, so I pretended we were going to Laloozee and that I wanted us to land on the lake there so that we could collect some water. I worried if we told her where we were really heading, she'd sabotage our plane. When she saw us heading north instead of south she became suspicious and decided to follow us. She'd been using the airstrip to take supplies up to the dam and had her small plane hidden there.'

'So is that why she was there when we crash-landed?' asked Gilbert.

'I believe so,' replied Fabio.

'How unfortunate for her we ran out of fuel,' laughed Gilbert.

'And the world's greatest flamingo detective landed in her village,' agreed Fabio.

About the Author

Laura James's love of storytelling began at an early age and led her to study Film and Writing for Young People at Bath Spa University. She has often thought she'd enjoy being a detective, with all the hunting for clues and asking lots of questions – sometimes even the right ones! Laura lives in the West Country.

About the Illustrator

Emily Fox is an illustrator based in Bristol. She graduated from Falmouth University and runs creative workshops for children as well as doing a lot of drawing! She loves to experiment with colour, funny stories and animals. Her favourite animals to draw are crocodiles, elephants and, of course, flamingos!

THE ADVENTURES OF

PUG!

AVAILABLE NOW

Read Fabio's other adventures

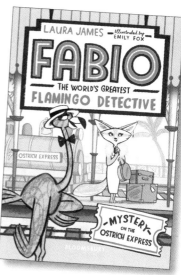

Available now